D0042938

GRANDPA CHATTERJI'S THIRD EYE

CALGARY PUBLIC LIBRARY

AUG – – 2006

EGMONT PRESS: ETHICAL PUBLISHING

Egmont Press is about turning writers into successful authors and children into passionate readers – producing books that enrich and entertain. As a responsible children's publisher, we go even further, considering the world in which our consumers are growing up.

Safety First
Naturally, all of our books meet legal safety requirements. But we go further than this; every book with play value is tested to the highest standards – if it fails, it's back to the drawing-board.

Made Fairly
We are working to ensure that the workers involved in our supply chain – the people that make our books – are treated with fairness and respect.

Responsible Forestry
We are committed to ensuring all our papers come from environmentally and socially responsible forest sources.

For more information, please visit our website at
www.egmont.co.uk/ethicalpublishing

Jamila Gavin

GRANDPA CHATTERJI'S THIRD EYE

Illustrated by Peter Bailey

EGMONT

Ask a grown-up to help you with the recipe at the back.

EGMONT
We bring stories to life

First published in Great Britain 2006
by Egmont UK Limited
239 Kensington High Street
London W8 6SA

Text copyright © 2006 Jamila Gavin
Illustrations © 2006 Peter Bailey

The moral rights of the author and illustrator have been asserted

ISBN 978 1 4052 1287 8
ISBN 1 4052 1287 X

1 3 5 7 9 10 8 6 4 2

A CIP catalogue record for this title is available from the British Library

Printed and bound in Great Britain by the CPI Group

All rights reserved. No part of this publication may be reproduced, stored
in a retrieval system, or transmitted, in any form or by any means, electronic,
mechanical, photocopying, recording or otherwise, without the prior permission
of the publisher and copyright owner.

Contents

Also by Jamila Gavin

Grandpa Chatterji
Grandpa's Indian Summer

Three Indian Princesses
Three Indian Goddesses
The Wheel of Surya

For older readers
The Blood Stone
Coram Boy

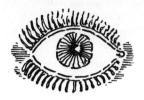

Cry Baby

Grandpa Chatterji sat in the aeroplane that was bringing him to Britain to see his grandchildren again. He was squashed right in the middle of the middle block, with no aisle on one side, and no window on the other. Hours had gone by. He would like to have got up and walked about, but he didn't want to disturb the other passengers, many of whom were sleeping soundly.

He didn't want to watch the in-flight film either, or listen to music on the headset, so he wriggled his toes, stretched his arms above him, and rotated his head.

'Bah . . . weh . . . yah . . .' A baby was bawling somewhere in front of him. She seemed to have been at it for ever.

'Hush, baby, hush!' he could hear her desperate mother trying to calm her.

A ripple of movement ran through the plane. People who were trying to sleep shuffled about and changed their positions as much as they could in the cramped seats. Those who were watching the film, or listening to music, wriggled their headsets, clamping them tighter on to their ears so as to block out the bawling.

'Bah . . . weh . . . yah . . . eh . . .!' the baby continued.

Grandpa saw a little head bobbing up and down, as Mother jogged the baby on her shoulder, patting her back and whispering soothing words.

Next to Mother, Father looked embarrassed. He was a new father. 'Can't you keep her quiet?' he asked with irritation.

'You try,' whispered Mother. 'I don't know what to do!'

So Father took the baby, holding her away from him, not wanting all its dribbling and tears to mess up his shirt. Bob, bob, bob! Father, too, could think of nothing else to do but bob the baby violently up and down.

'Bah . . . weh . . . yah . . . ahhh . . .' the baby cried even louder and struggled with arms outstretched to go back to Mummy.

Mother fumbled for a bottle. Back came baby, clasping Mother round her neck in a stranglehold. 'Bah . . . weh . . . yah . . .' she howled. 'Bah . . . weh . . . gulp!' The crying stopped abruptly as the teat of the bottle was pushed into her mouth. 'Splat!' The baby jerked her head away and with mouth wide open began her bawling again. Mother looked as if she too could cry. She thrust the baby back to Father.

From his seat, Grandpa could see the little head bobbing first with Father, then disappearing as if under a wave, and reappearing with Mother.

And so, back and forth the baby went between mother and father, wailing and screaming, till now everyone was awake. Passengers sighed with patient fortitude, trying not to feel irritated by the persistent cries. Even ear plugs didn't help.

'Oh dear,' sighed Grandpa Chatterji to himself. 'We have many more hours to go. Perhaps I can do something to help.' He uncurled his feet and tapped his neighbour. 'Excuse me!' he smiled apologetically. The neighbour tapped the person sitting next to him, and jerked his head in Grandpa's direction as if to say, 'It's not my fault I've woken you from your sleep. The gentleman here wants to get out.'

With a lot of heaving and puffing, the two passengers on his right tipped themselves out of their seats and allowed Grandpa Chatterji to wriggle free. Then they settled themselves back as quickly as they could and resumed their sleeping positions.

'Thank you, thank you, so sorry to have disturbed you,' Grandpa muttered, and made his way down the aisle towards the bawling child.

Mother was violently rocking her child to and fro, while Father made vain attempts to tickle baby's toes and make funny faces. But still baby yelled. 'Bah . . . yeh . . . weh . . .'

'Oh dearie me!' Grandpa Chatterji paused beside the desperate family. 'Why don't you let me walk your baby up and down a bit. It will give you some rest. Eh?' He cocked his head, smiled his smile of sublimity, gazed at them with his deep as ocean eyes, and held out his arms.

Mother and Father looked up at him like startled rabbits. Father frowned and looked at Mother. Was this a mad man? What did he think he was doing, interfering in their business.

But they had failed to stop their baby crying, and people were now glaring at them with accusing faces, as if they were such bad parents. Mother and Father exchanged silent messages with each other. Could they hand over their baby to a stranger? Yet, what harm could come of it? After all, there they all were flying high at 33,000 feet, and he couldn't exactly run away with her.

'I'm a grandfather,' murmured Grandpa soothingly. 'I'm used to children. I already have six grandchildren. I'm on my way to visit two of them in England, Neetu and Sanjay. Lovely children. This is your first baby, yes?'

They nodded blankly. 'And last,' muttered Father under his breath.

'So you see, I'm used to babies. Come, let me take her for a walk, and you can get some sleep.'

Father looked at Mother. Mother looked at Father. Baby bawled loud as ever. Passengers sighed with exasperation. Father nodded in surrender. 'Well, if you think you can do something . . .' he muttered grudgingly.

'Thank you, sir. It's very kind.' Mother passed her baby parcel to Father, who handed her to Grandpa Chatterji.

Grandpa folded the baby into his arms, and beamed down into its furious little face. 'There, there, there . . .' he rocked her gently. 'Let's go for a walk, shall we?'

'Bah . . . weh . . . yah . . .' Baby screamed, as Grandpa trundled off down the aisle, the wails diminishing into the distance. Father shrugged almost triumphantly.

'There's always someone who thinks they know better. He'll soon be back.'

Grandpa Chatterji reached the tail end of the plane. Baby was still crying and spluttering and was so red in the face that he thought she would explode. Grandpa loosened the warm, zipped-up-to-the-chin baby suit which seemed to be cooking the baby, and breathed cool air down her neck.

He rocked her gently instead of bouncing her up and down. He cooed into her ear with his deep, husky voice, and sang a Bengali lullaby. The wail began to be punctuated with gasps for breath. Instead of one long, unbroken sound, it stopped, started, stopped again, and started, but a little less explosively. Then silence.

Baby looked up with great round tear-brimming blue eyes, into Grandpa's dark brown kindly gaze. 'Bah . . .' she started . . . then softened it to 'Gooo.'

'Goo Goo!' chuckled Grandpa, tickling her under the chin. He gazed back into her deep blue eyes as if he looked into the first ocean of creation; into the sea of milk from which the whole world had come into existence.

'Gurgle, gurgle,' warbled Baby like a little bird. Then her large blue eyes blinked as the tears dried. Perhaps as she looked into the worlds of his eyes, she saw love and patience and wonderment at the miracle of her creation.

Grandpa Chatterji patted Baby like a little drum, with a gentle rhythmic hand, beating in time to her heartbeat. She stared

– not just into his two eyes, but perhaps into his third eye, which only a newly created being could see glimmering in his forehead.

She blinked again, but more slowly and heavily. The lids closed and opened. The next time she blinked, her eyelids stayed shut and all the tension went out of her body as she gave way to sleep.

'Are you a magician?' whispered the air steward. 'I wish you'd fly with us more often.'

Grandpa smiled. 'Travel is so exhausting for little ones,' he said, 'but she will sleep now.'

Still rocking her gently, Grandpa Chatterji

walked back down the long, darkened cabin.
People lolled in slumber, some with heads
thrown back and mouths open, others
leaning up against their neighbours, or
curled up against their pillows.

He reached Mother and Father. Father
was asleep with headphones still clamped to
his ears. But Mother looked up with wide
anxious eyes as Grandpa arrived. Baby was
now breathing in some deep, peaceful place
where nothing could reach her to wake her
up. Grandpa gently offered her into Mother's
arms. 'I think she was a bit too hot,' he
whispered. 'We're not in England yet!'

'Thank you!' Mother mouthed her words.
'Thank you.'

He made his way back to his seat.

'Excuse me! I'm so sorry to disturb you,'

he said, disturbing his fellow passengers with mumbled apologies. 'Sorry. So sorry. I beg your pardon. Forgive me. Thank you.' Grandpa managed to get back into his seat. Settling back, he closed his eyes.

Anyone passing by could have thought he was sleeping, but they may not have

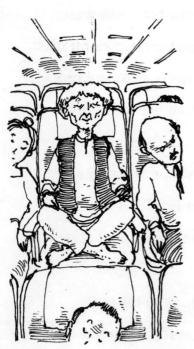

noticed that he had tucked his bare feet up into a cross-legged position, with his arms resting on his knees. Though he looked so still and quiet, Grandpa Chatterji was seeing with his third eye, his inner eye, his eye of thought and contemplation.

His mind created a beautiful pale lotus, floating on tranquil water. He felt that he was floating too. He began to see images, as if reflected in the water. He saw his daughter's house, where he was going for a holiday, and the street lined with maple trees. He saw his grandchildren, Neetu and Sanjay, and smiled fondly. They were both in school, trying to concentrate. But he knew they were thinking about him, just as he was thinking about them.

'I'll be with you soon,' he sighed, then he too slipped into a deep sleep.

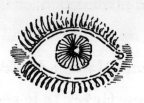

Grandpa's Back

'Grandpa Chatterji

Matterji

Batterji

Hatterji

Fatterji.'

Sanjay had been muttering under his breath all day at school.

'What did you say?' asked his teacher, Mrs Morgan.

'My grandpa's coming to see us again, all the way from India. That's probably him now,' he cried excitedly, as they heard the distant roar of an aeroplane overhead.

But Sanjay had been saying that all day. Every time a plane went over he shouted, 'That's my Grandpa Chatterji, flying in!'

'He can't be in all those aeroplanes,' said his best friend Ross, after the fifth time.

'He's in one of them,' grinned Sanjay, 'and he'll bring presents for us.'

He went on muttering, as he stared at the long thin streak of silver threading across the sky heading towards the airport.

'Grandpa Chatterji

Matterji

Batterji

Hatterji

Fatterji.'

'Is he fat?' asked Ross.

'Of course not,' laughed Sanjay.

'Then why are you saying he's fat?'

'I'm not. There's nothing the matterji with him, he's not batterji, he doesn't wear a hatterji, and he isn't fatterji, it just rhymes with Chatterji, that's all.'

'Oh!' murmured Ross, and he too started
to mutter,

'Grandpa Chatterji

Isn't fatterji

The matterji is that

Sanjay's batterji.'

'No I'm not!' protested Sanjay.

'Sanjay, are you chattering again? Get
on with your work,' said their teacher,
sternly.

'Sanjay Chatterbox!' hissed Ross
sniggering into his hand.

Neetu, sitting in another classroom, had
trouble concentrating too. She wondered if
Grandpa Chatterji had come with his
baggage roll, which had everything in it; his
bed, his clothes, his toothbrush, his hairbrush

and comb, his spare shirt and pyjamas and his white, cotton dhoti. She wondered if he had brought his old, worn carpet, on which he sat to meditate. She wondered if he still stood on his head. After all, he was older now.

When school was over, Mum was waiting for Neetu and Sanjay at the gate. She looked excited. She hadn't seen her father for over a year, and oh, how she had missed him.

'Come on, you two. Grandpa's home.'

'Wonderful,' shouted Neetu. 'Let's hurry.'

'I told you, Ross!' Sanjay slapped his friend on the back. 'And he's sure to have a present for me!'

Mum, Neetu and Sanjay set off home. But Sanjay could

never just walk. He had to
hop, he had to walk
backwards, he had to
dart about like a fighter
plane, with his arms
outstretched, making very
loud zoom zooming noises.

The black cat on the wall stretched and
arched its back as they came near.

'Hello, pussycat,' murmured Neetu,
giving it a hug and a stroke.

'Hello, Pussyji,' said Sanjay, zooming up
to her. 'Grandpa's back again. He might
have presents, isn't that great?'

'Purrr,' agreed the black cat, pushing her
head into his hand, and he tickled her ears
murmuring, 'catterji, matterji, batterji,
chatterji.'

When they reached their street, Neetu walked faster and faster, leaving Mum and Sanjay behind. She broke into a run. 'I'm going to see Grandpa first!' she cried.

'Wait for me!' wailed Sanjay, and chased after her.

'Don't disturb Grandpa,' Mum called after them. 'He's resting after his long flight.'

But her words were lost, as Neetu and Sanjay raced down the road, up to their house, and inside the door.

The house was silent. Dad wasn't yet home from work. They looked for any sign of Grandpa.

'He IS here,' whispered Neetu. 'Look!'

Just inside the door was a pair of Indian sandals. Grandpa always took off his shoes when he came into a house.

'He IS here, look!' Sanjay pointed to a black rolled-up umbrella in the umbrella stand. He drew it out and held it as if it were a magic wand.

A smell of lotus flowers wafted through the house, and they saw a thin coil of scented smoke rising from a joss stick, burning in a holder on the mantelpiece.

'Grandpa's back!'

They looked up the flight of stairs. They knew Grandpa was to have the guest room. Sanjay began to creep up the stairs, muttering under his breath, 'oner-ji, twoer-ji, threer-ji, fourer-ji,

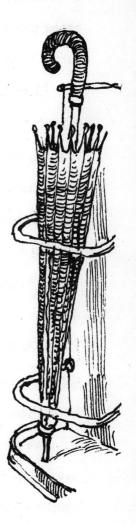

Sanjayji wants to see Grandpa Chatterji.'

'No,' hissed Neetu. 'Mummy said we mustn't disturb him.'

'I won't disturb him, I'll just peep.'

But Mum arrived and shook her head. 'Let Grandpa rest for a bit. He's very tired. You never get much sleep on an aeroplane. He'll come down when he's ready. Come and have your tea.'

Neetu and Sanjay followed Mum into the kitchen. They gobbled down some sandwiches, and gulped down some juice, then Mum said, 'Go and play quietly, while I get on with the supper.' She looked thoughtfully at her vegetable basket. 'I think I'll give Grandpa spinach and lightly spiced potatoes. Nothing too rich after his long journey.'

Neetu got out her favourite book and tried to read, but Sanjay wouldn't let her. He jumped over her, he flicked her hair, he sat on her back, he turned the page before she had read it, and he whispered in her ear: 'Grandpa Chatterji, matterji, batterji, hatterji, fatterji, thinnerji, I think you're sillyji.'

Usually Neetu ignored him. She knew that that was the best way to deal with troublesome brothers. He would get bored and leave her alone. So she fixed her eyes on the page, and went on trying to read.

Sanjay did get bored. Giving his sister a final prod, he left her alone and went to the bottom of the stairs. He thought no one was looking, so he put one foot on the bottom stair, then bit by bit, he went slowly and quietly up to the top.

But Neetu was looking out of the corner of her eye. She slammed the book shut, and ran to the bottom of the stairs. 'Sanjay!' Neetu whispered sharply. 'Come down. Mum says we mustn't . . .' But suddenly, Neetu couldn't help it; she too was tiptoeing up the stairs.

They pressed their ears to the door of Grandpa's room and listened. But there was not one sound.

Sanjay's hand went to the door knob.

Neetu frowned and shook her head. 'No

Sanjay,' she mouthed.

But Sanjay took no notice. Slowly, quietly, he turned the handle. The door opened a crack; wide enough for a peep. They peeped.

There was Grandpa Chatterji. His eyes were closed, his face was serene, and he was upside down, standing on his curly grey head.

Suddenly, one eye opened; one deep, brown eye. Then another eye, then a big grin spread across his upside-down face. Grinning too, Neetu and Sanjay dropped to their knees and crawled across the floor.

'Are you resting, Grandpa?' asked Neetu softly, resting her cheek beside him.

'Yes, after such a long flight, I feel much calmer upside down.'

'Me too. I've been practising, Grandpa,' whispered Neetu, and stood on her head next to him.

'Me too,' said Sanjay, but couldn't quite get two feet off the ground.

★   ★   ★

Dad came home. The house was silent. He went quickly to the kitchen. Mum was cooking. 'Where is everyone? Where's your father? Where are the children?'

'Papa's resting, and the kids are playing . . . aren't they?' She, too, now realised how quiet everything was. Neetu's book was lying abandoned, and there was no sound from Sanjay. That was very unusual. Everything was too quiet.

Mum and Dad went to the bottom of the stairs. Silence. They crept up to the top. There was no one on the landing. They went along to Grandpa's room. Mum knocked very softly and politely, 'Papaji?'

'Come in, come in!' Grandpa Chatterji's voice called out.

Mum and Dad opened the door. There was Grandpa Chatterji, Neetu and Sanjay, all upside down.

'We're being bats,' said Sanjay. 'Grandpa Chatterji, matterji, hatterji, batterji.'

'Oh dear,' Dad looked at Mum with a sigh. 'Now I know your father's back.'

Sanjay's Present

Neetu and Sanjay stared at Grandpa's
luggage roll.

Neetu rolled it across the room. Sanjay
sat on top of it, bouncing up and down.

'You've got new stickers,' said Sanjay,
examining all the travel stickers. 'Mumbai,
Chennai, Bangalore, Calcutta . . .' Sanjay
slowly read out each one. 'Dubai . . .
London!'

'Can we see what's inside?' asked Neetu, trying not to sound too eager.

'Have you got presents for us?' demanded Sanjay, sounding very eager.

'Mmmm,' murmured Grandpa Chatterji. 'You can help me to unpack.' He undid the thick leather straps, and unrolled the khaki baggage roll. It had flaps tied over his belongings. He untied the flaps. The children knelt on the floor, one on each side. What would he have for them this time?

'Are you sleeping on the floor again?' asked Sanjay.

'It's the most comfortable place for me!' smiled Grandpa. 'Most beds are too soft.'

'I don't know how you can bring so little,' cried Neetu wonderingly, as Grandpa laid his clothes out on the bed. 'Dad takes a whole suitcase full when he's only going away for two days.'

'Two days, two weeks, two years, it's all the same to me,' said Grandpa. 'Wear one, wash one, that's my motto.' So out came two pairs of trousers, two pyjama sets, two shirts, two vests, two pants, two pairs of socks, two pullovers and a waistcoat. In the pocket at one end, he pulled out his tooth mug, toothbrush, his shaving things, brush and comb all wrapped in a towel. At the other end, he pulled out a waistcoat, a woolly hat and some handkerchiefs.

'I suppose you'll have to wash something every day then,' sighed Neetu at the thought of it.

'I wash myself every day, so all I do is wash out my clothes too,' replied Grandpa, rubbing his hands.

'Are the presents underneath?' cried
Sanjay, wriggling his fingers beneath the
sheet and blanket, which made up Grandpa's
bed.

'Still the same boy,' chuckled Grandpa,
prodding him in the ribs.

'You've brought your carpet,' whispered
Neetu softly, lifting it out of the baggage roll
and spreading it out. She remembered
Grandpa's rug from before. It was his
thinking rug.

'Oh yes,' smiled Grandpa. 'We will sit on
it and meditate.'

'But we can have our presents first, can't
we, Grandpa?' asked Sanjay, still rifling
through Grandpa's luggage roll. Suddenly,
underneath the blanket, he felt a long, flat,

hard package, all wrapped in newspaper and
bound with string. He tugged it out. 'Is this a
present?'

Grandpa looked very solemn.

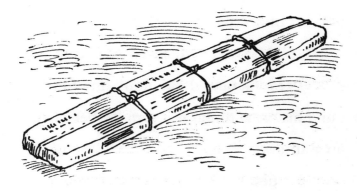

'Sanjay!' exclaimed Neetu sharply.
'You're being very rude. That might be
something precious. Put it back. It's
Grandpa's.'

'Is it?' persisted Sanjay, holding it close.

'Give it to me, Sanjay,' said Grandpa in
a stern voice. Sanjay gave it to him.

Grandpa continued unpacking. 'This is a

new saree for Mummy, and this is a raw silk waistcoat for Daddy, and this . . .' said Grandpa slowly, holding up the hard, flat, long package, 'is very precious, Sanjay, but . . .' and with a huge grin, he handed it back, 'it is for you, O beloved grandson.'

'Oh thank you, thank you!' and Sanjay flung his arms round his grandfather. 'Can I open it now?'

'Yes, yes, but be careful. Don't damage it.'

Neetu waited patiently.

As Sanjay began to pull off the string, and tear aside the newspaper, Grandpa dipped his hand into a side pocket of his bedroll. 'And this, my darling granddaughter, is for you.' He pulled out a small red and gold box, and handed it to

Neetu with a respectful bow.

'What IS it?' Sanjay sounded
disappointed. He had finally unwrapped his
gift, and all he could see were thin sheets of
brown and black paper, stuck to long thin
sticks of bamboo. Lying on top was a ball of
bright yellow string. He screwed up his face.
It looked . . . well . . . Sanjay frowned . . .
rather boring.

'What's THIS?' asked Neetu as she
opened her red and gold box. 'Oh, Grandpa,
is this really for me? She lifted out first a gold
bracelet and then a fine gold chain, all rolled
and plaited.

'Here, let me put it on for you.' Grandpa
took the gold chain. Neetu lifted up her hair
while he circled it round her neck and
fastened the clasp. 'Gold for my golden girl,'

he murmured happily. Then she held out her right arm, for him to clasp the bracelet round her wrist.

She ran to a mirror and stared at herself. 'I look like a princess!' she cried.

'You're lucky,' grumbled Sanjay. 'You like your present.'

'And don't you like yours?' asked Grandpa, fixing him with a long deep brown gaze.

'I don't know what it is,' groaned Sanjay. 'What am I meant to do with bits of paper? I'm bigger now. That's for little children. I was hoping you might bring me a gun or a spear.'

Grandpa shook his head sadly and tut tutted. 'Dearie me, no! Why would I bring things to do with killing? I've brought you something to do with life and living, flying and touching the sky. Come on! Let's go out and discover what this present is.'

They thudded down stairs, Sanjay leaping two at a time.

'Where are you off to?' asked Dad, coming to see what was going on.

'We're going to demonstrate Sanjay's present,' said Grandpa.

'But, Papa, you should be resting after your journey,' cried Mum, rushing out too.

'I've rested. I'm full of energy. We're only going out for a while!' cried Grandpa, wriggling his long bony feet into his sandals.

'Don't get up to mischief,' begged Mum.

'We won't!' Grandpa reassured her. 'We'll be good.'

'I've heard that before,' groaned Dad.

'Have you got your present, Sanjay? You're going to find out what it is.'

Grandpa opened the gate and strode off, with Neetu and Sanjay running to keep up. They went down the road, passed the black cat, which arched his back and purred, over the traffic lights, down the main street, and towards the park.

'Can we play on the swings?' asked Sanjay, looking longingly at the playground with its swings and slide.

'Later!' cried Grandpa. 'Come on!'

They rushed on. They came to the pond, where the ducks quacked and splashed and dived for newts. When they saw Grandpa, Neetu and Sanjay, they flapped out of the water and waddled over, nipping their fingers, demanding food, and making such a din. 'Oh Grandpa, can we stay and feed the ducks?' begged Neetu.

'Later!' shouted Grandpa, bounding on.

They left the smooth lawns of the park behind, and the swings. The ground grew rougher, and rose up and up. It became a hill with little paths winding among gorse bushes and wild brambles. It was quite steep. That didn't stop Grandpa. He went springing up like a mountain goat.

'Wait for me!' wailed Sanjay.

At last they reached the top. The sky was

a summer evening blue, just beginning to darken. Suddenly the air was as fresh as a cool drink, and it was so high, they could see the whole town spread below them. It was almost like being a bird. Grandpa stopped. 'I think we've arrived!'

'What do we do now, Grandpa?' asked Neetu, panting up behind him.

Grandpa licked the pad of his first finger and held it up. 'Which way is the wind blowing?' He licked it again, and turned the other way. 'Ah! We have a southerly wind.'

Neetu licked a finger and held it above her head. 'How can you tell?'

'Because if you hold your wet finger up in the direction the wind is coming from, you feel it go cold.'

'Why have we come all the way up here

with my present?' gasped Sanjay, holding his sides. 'What are we going to do now?'

'We are going to have fun,' said Grandpa Chatterji, and he chuckled with enthusiasm. 'Come on, come on! Open it up!'

Sanjay opened the parcel. There were the thin sheets of brown and black paper, edged with bamboo. There was the bright green ball of string. Grandpa knelt down on the ground and fitted the bamboo rods together. The children gazed intently, as the thin sheets of paper began to become something.

'I think I know what it is!' exclaimed Neetu.

Grandpa attached the end of the ball of string to a small hook. Then he stood up and shook the construction gently.

'It's a kite!' cried Neetu. 'Grandpa

brought you a kite!'

'It's more than a kite,' said Grandpa, and he unfolded a last piece which Sanjay hadn't noticed.

'It's an eagle!' yelled Sanjay.

The kite was an eagle. It had long spreading wings and a powerful eagle's head, with a curved beak and bright hard eyes. Grandpa handed Sanjay the ball of green string and unwound an arm's-length of it, then, turning north, he lifted the kite up in the air. 'When I let go of the kite, Sanjay, just give the string a little tug to help it catch the wind, then be ready to unwind the ball and give it enough length to fly higher and higher.'

Grandpa tossed the kite upwards. A southerly wind caught the eagle's wings.

Grandpa gave a little tug on the string. The kite rose higher. 'Unwind a bit more!' he yelled, leaping up and down. Sanjay unwound more string, and the kite rose even higher.

'It's flying! The eagle is flying! Now do you like your present, Sanjay?'

'I love it! Thank you, Grandpa. Grandpa Chatterji,

Chatter Chatter Chatterji,' exclaimed
Sanjay, his eyes fixed on the kite. He felt he
was up there too; he imagined he was an
eagle, flying over the world. It looked like a
chess board; all the people, the houses, the
cars and lorries, looked like little toys; yet his
eagle eye was as sharp as a microscope; it
could see the white flash of a rabbit's tail; the
flutter of grass as a dormouse sped for cover,
and the grey weasel paralysed among the
rocks.

But suddenly, 'Oh look!' Sanjay was
dismayed. 'It's coming down.' He tugged at
the string, as the kite spiralled downwards as
if wounded.

'Here, give it to me.' Grandpa snatched the ball of string from Sanjay's hand. He began running along the ridge, tugging the string as he went. The kite began to rise up again.

'Look Sanjay! Look at your eagle,' cried Grandpa excitedly. 'Look at its wings, feathering out in the wind. Go, go!' he shouted. 'Fly! Be an eagle. Go hunting over the rocks and moors. Watch out rabbits, weasels and little mice! Here comes the eagle with his sharp, curved beak, ready to swoop down and eat you up.'

'Can I have it back now?' cried Sanjay,

leaping up and down.

'In a minute, in a minute,' yelled
Grandpa. 'It's just beginning to fly really well.'

The kite twisted, and then turned its beak
skywards again. It rose up and up. Grandpa
unravelled the string even more, and soon the
eagle was just a speck, high in the sky, wafting
this way and that.

'Now can I have it back?' begged Sanjay,
longing to hold the string.

'Yes – but just let me . . .' Grandpa
muttered, still clutching the end of the string.

Neetu and Sanjay watched the kite for a
long time. They watched Grandpa running up
and down the ridge, tugging the kite and
playing with the wind.

'Please can I have it now?' pleaded Sanjay.

'Soon, soon! I just want to be sure it's

working properly,' Grandpa answered breathlessly.

The children got tired of standing, and sat down under a small blackthorn tree to wait. They waited and waited.

'When can I have it?' Sanjay moaned again. 'It's MY present!'

They waited and waited. But Grandpa seemed to forget all about them. He stood, staring up at the kite far, far away on the end of the string, as if his mind was up there too.

Suddenly, there was an extra puff of wind. It caught Grandpa by surprise, and tugged the ball of string out of his hands. Down the hill it rolled and, as it rolled it unravelled, and as it unravelled, the kite broke free and joyfully soared away, twisting and bucking on the currents of air.

Grandpa scrambled down the slope after
the string. 'Quick, catch it, catch it!'

Neetu and Sanjay sprang to their feet,
and also went tumbling and slithering down
the hill, trying to grasp the ball of string, but
as it rolled, it unravelled even more and
soon there was no ball at all,
just the end of the
string, hovering
in the

air, trailing away out of
reach.

Grandpa jumped and leapt, his fingers

trying desperately to catch it, but it was no use. The three of them stood watching helplessly, as the kite drifted away over the park, with its long green string trailing behind.

'Isn't it magnificent,' sighed Grandpa with admiration. 'What a marvellous kite. Who would have thought it could fly so high.'

'But that's my present gone!' protested Sanjay.

'Will we be able to get it back?' asked Neetu.

'Who knows,' Grandpa shook his head ruefully. 'That kite's got a mind of its own. But don't worry Sanjay, I'll get you another, I promise.'

'But that one was from India. Another won't be as good,' said Sanjay, mournfully.

Grandpa patted his grandson comfortingly. 'We'll see, we'll see. Come on, let's go and you can play on the swings.'

Sanjay shook his head; one minute he had hated his present, then he loved his present, and now it was gone – and Grandpa didn't seem to mind at all. With disappointed steps, Sanjay trudged back down the hill behind Neetu and Grandpa Chatterji. Every now and then they glanced upwards into the sky, to see where the kite had gone. But all they saw was a flock of birds wheeling in the evening sky.

While Neetu and Sanjay played on the swings, the slide and

the roundabout, Grandpa Chatterji sat cross-legged on the grass. He rested his arms over his knees, and closed his eyes.

'Are you meditating, Grandpa?' Neetu had got tired of playing, and joined her grandfather. 'I'm so glad you've come back to visit us,' she said, sitting next to him.

'Nothing makes me more happy than to be with my grandchildren,' murmured Grandpa. 'Now take up the lotus position, like me.'

Neetu crossed her legs, straightened her back and rested her arms over her knees. 'What are we thinking about, Grandpa?' she asked.

'We are thinking about the kite. We are getting into the mind of the eagle.'

She closed her eyes, and soon her mind

was up with the eagle kite, bobbing in the wind, flying nearly as high as the pale white moon that gradually appeared in the sky.

After a while, Sanjay came to see what they were doing. He sat on the other side of Grandpa, crossed his legs and leaned his arms on top of his knees. 'What are we doing, Grandpa?'

'We are flying with the kite. Did you know you have three eyes: two on the outside, and one on the inside? Close your two eyes, and only look with your third eye; your inner eye. Fly with the kite in your mind, up in the clouds, over the treetops. Look! Can you see it? What fun it's having.'

Sanjay tried, but gave up. 'I can't see anything with my eyes shut. I haven't got three eyes.' He opened his two eyes and scanned the empty sky. There was nothing; not even a bird or an aeroplane. 'This is stupid,' he said sullenly. 'Can we go home now?' And he jumped to his feet, feeling cross.

'In a minute, in a minute,' said Grandpa. 'You've got to have trust, Sanjay. You didn't think you would like your present, but you did. Now you think you'll never see it again. But who knows?'

Sanjay wandered off in the direction of

home, and soon, Grandpa and Neetu were hurrying along behind him.

'Oh dear what is the matterji,

Sanjay's cross with poor Grandpa Chatterji

His kite flew away and may not come backerji,

Nobody knows where it's gone,' Neetu recited.

'What's happened?' exclaimed Mum, when she saw the children's gloomy faces.

'Grandpa gave me a kite and lost it,' muttered Sanjay, and wandered off to his Play Station.

'It's safely lost,' insisted Grandpa reassuringly. 'We'll find it.'

'We tried to meditate and make it come back, but it didn't,' said Neetu, and went off to find her book.

'I told Sanjay not to worry. It will all come right,' said Grandpa serenely. 'He'll see. Have you got a cup of tea for me, by any chance?'

'There's always a cup of tea for you, Papa – even when you're bad!' said his daughter, taking his arm.

That night, before he lay down on his bedroll, Grandpa Chatterji sat on his thinking rug. He sat cross-legged and straight-backed, with his arms resting across his knees, and his thumb and third finger touching lightly. He lifted his head and closed his eyes. Then he breathed deeply. 'Om . . . Om . . .'

As Neetu drifted off to sleep, she heard the syllable 'Om' carrying her like a great wave on the back of the ocean.

Sanjay woke early the next morning. He
could hear Grandpa having his bucket bath –
which he preferred to a bath or a shower. He
liked to stand in the bath, fill his plastic
bucket with luke-warm water, slosh it all over
himself with a mug, then scrub with soap,
and rinse by sloshing it all over himself
again. 'That way, you don't waste water,' he
had told them. Then he brushed his teeth and
gargled with salt water very loudly.

Sanjay rolled out of bed and looked out
of his window across the back garden.

Suddenly, something caught his eye. It
was a long piece of green string trailing
among the branches of the sycamore tree at
the bottom. His eye followed it upwards

among the branches; higher and higher, until
. . . he saw something brown and black,
fluttering gently among the leaves;
something with a head, with beady eyes, and
a beak.

'GRANDPA!' he shrieked, and everyone
leapt from their beds as if the house was on
fire. 'GRANDPA!' He rushed downstairs,
followed by Mum, Dad and Neetu in their
night clothes – and finally followed by
Grandpa with a towel round his middle and
his long grey hair dripping round his
shoulders.

'What is it, Sanjay? What's the matter?'
they cried.

Sanjay pulled open the kitchen door and
raced outside. 'Look!'

They all stood on the lawn and stared.

Dangling from the branches
was the end of a piece of green string.
Their eyes followed the string up and
up until, there, fluttering high among
the branches was Sanjay's kite.

'It's here! It came back!'

'You mean, this is the kite you lost
up on the hill, and it's flown all the way
back here?' gasped Dad
disbelievingly. 'You're having me on!'

'It's true, Dad,' cried Neetu.

'Didn't I tell you!' cried Grandpa
jubilantly. 'I'll just climb up and get it.'

'Oh no, you don't,' snapped Dad,
pulling him back. 'I will.'

'Get dressed first,' wailed Mum. 'Look
at you, Papa, you're half naked. You'll
catch your death of cold!'

But her words fell
on deaf ears as Dad
and Grandpa raced
across the lawn.

He didn't like to
admit it, but Dad
enjoyed climbing up
that tree. He was like a
boy again, easing
himself up from branch
to branch, looking for
footholds, until, at last, he
was within reach of the kite.

'Careful! Don't tear it. It looks
as if it's in one piece,' Grandpa
yelled instructions from below.

Dad was very careful. Wedging his
back against the trunk, and his feet up

against a large branch, he undid the kite from the string and gently freed it from the twigs that had held it to the tree.

By this time, Grandpa was halfway up the tree too. 'Pass it down to me,' he cried. 'You'll need two hands to get down.'

So Dad passed the kite down to Grandpa, who passed it down to Mum who, even in her dressing gown, had climbed on to the very lowest branch, ready to help.

Neetu lifted Sanjay up in her arms. 'Take the kite from Mum, Sanjay,' she cried, giving him a heave.

Sanjay took the kite from his mother. Tenderly, he held it out and looked at its wings and the eagle head. 'You came back to me,' he whispered, and he shut his eyes.

Suddenly, he realised he was seeing with

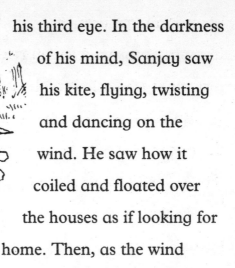 his third eye. In the darkness of his mind, Sanjay saw his kite, flying, twisting and dancing on the wind. He saw how it coiled and floated over the houses as if looking for home. Then, as the wind dropped, the kite floated down, down, down and landed in the tree at the bottom of their garden. There it waited for Sanjay to wake up. 'Next time you fly away, take me with you,' sighed Sanjay happily.

'After breakfast, we'll go and fly the kite again,' said Grandpa.

'But this time, I'LL hold the kite,' said Sanjay.

'And this time, I'm coming too,'

pronounced Dad firmly.

'I think we'll all go,' said Mum.

'Try

Fly

High

Sky,' muttered Sanjay, dreamily.

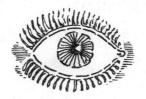

Grandpa Leicester's Party

The phone rang. It was Grandpa Leicester, calling all the way from Leicester. 'I want to hold a party for your father,' he told Mum. 'Are you free next Saturday? I'll ask a few friends round – just a little welcome sort of a thing.'

'That's very kind of you,' said Mum. 'We'd love to come, and I'm sure my father will feel most honoured.'

Since Grandpa Chatterji had arrived, they had woken up each morning to the sound of 'Om', as he did his breathing exercises, and the sloshing, splashing, gargling and snorting coming from the bathroom. But this morning, the morning of Grandpa Leicester's party, it was the smell which woke them up; a delicious, mouth-watering smell.

Mum hurried downstairs. 'What is going on?' she wondered. The smell was coming from the kitchen, even though the door was shut.

She opened it, and a cloud of steam and smoke streamed out. It was as if a steam engine had come inside. Somewhere through the haze, she made out a figure, bare to the waist, wearing just a dhoti, with a ladle in hand, bent over an open pot like some kind of magician. He stirred and tossed further ingredients into the pot, with a great splattering and spluttering.

'Papa!' wailed Mum, in dismay. 'What on earth are you up to? We're supposed to be getting ready to go to Leicester for the party. Why are you cooking?'

'I'm just making a few pakoras, my dear. You know how Grandpa Leicester loves my pakoras – and we can't go empty-handed.'

'We aren't going empty-handed,' protested Mum. 'I bought a big box of Grandpa Leicester's favourite Ambala sweets. Leave this – and get dressed. We mustn't be late. You know what Grandpa Leicester's like.'

'Go, go! Put on that lovely silk saree I bought you from Varanasi. You all get dressed – and get the children ready, while I finish this and then I'll get ready too,' Grandpa said cheerily.

'But look at the mess! I hate leaving my kitchen looking like this,' Mum protested.

'Don't worry. I'll clear up. I promise,' and he chucked another handful of vegetables into the batter. A puff of steam hissed into the air, and Mum fled, slamming the door behind her.

Some time later, they were all dressed: Dad in his smartest suit, white shirt and silk tie, Mum in her new purple silk saree, with its

gold embroidered border, which Grandpa
had brought her all the way from India,
Neetu in her very best pink and white dress,
with the frilly collar and sleeves, and
Grandpa's present – her gold necklace and
bracelet, and Sanjay, looking like a little
grown-up gentleman in his black trousers,
white shirt with a bow-tie, and black
waistcoat.

But where was Grandpa?

Dad looked at his watch. 'We've got to go now, or we'll be late, and you know how Father hates us being late. Do hurry him up,' he begged Mum.

'Oh dear, I last saw him cooking in the kitchen, still wearing his dhoti,' and Mum was about to yell into the kitchen when suddenly, there was a resplendent Grandpa Chatterji at the top of the stairs. His grey curls were all brushed and shiny, and he was wearing pure white linen Indian pyjamas, with a white linen tunic and a dark grey waistcoat.

He hurried downstairs. 'Come, come, come! What are you all doing, standing about? We'll be late. Haven't you got the car out yet? You know how Grandpa Leicester hates unpunctuality. What does he always say? Punctuality is the courtesy of kings! Eh?'

Dad threw up his eyes with exasperation.

'Oh!' Grandpa gasped, and dashed to the kitchen.

'Now where's he going?' groaned Dad.

'Nearly forgot my pakoras,' grinned Grandpa. He reappeared, dangling a plastic bag in his hand.

'That goes into the boot,' said Dad, firmly taking the bag from him. 'I don't want my car smelling of pakoras!'

As carefully as they could, they arranged themselves in Dad's little red car, trying not to crease their clothes, and off they went, heading down the motorway for Leicester.

At last, they turned into the street where Grandpa Leicester lived, and knew

immediately which house was his. It was decked with green, orange and white flags, all fluttering merrily.

'The colours of India,' cried Grandpa Chatterji with appreciation.

There was Grandpa Leicester waiting for them, looking very smart and sleek in his new, pale brown summer suit.

'Hello, good sir!' exclaimed Grandpa Chatterji, rushing up to Grandpa Leicester, holding out his plastic bag of pakoras.

'Welcome back, good sir!' intoned Grandpa Leicester, who winced as Grandpa Chatterji flung his arms round him and gave him a big hug. 'Mind my suit,' he pleaded feebly.

'Here, I made these specially for you,' cried Grandpa Chatterji, thrusting the bag of pakoras into his hands. 'I know how you love them!'

Grandpa Leicester held the offering at arms' length, and Grandpa Chatterji didn't seem to notice the look on his face, as if he'd been given something out of the dustbin.

'And I've brought you some Ambala sweets,' cried Mum, embracing her father-in-law. 'I think they're your favourites.'

'Quite right, quite right! Thank you, my dear,' smiled Grandpa Leicester happily, and steered them all into the house.

A lot of people had already gathered; men with twirling moustaches, ladies swishing in wonderful sarees, and lots of children darting between the grown-ups, like minnows in a stream. They all dived in, and soon scattered into the house and garden.

Sanjay caught a glimpse of the table in the dining room. It was the biggest table he had ever seen. It was bigger than the whole of their front room and it was laden with all sorts of things to eat and nibble.

He rushed in eagerly. The first thing he saw was a golden box of chocolates, which one of the guests had brought for Grandpa Leicester. Sanjay loved chocolates, but he knew he didn't always like the fillings, so he took out one after the other, unwrapped it carefully, took a little bite, and if it was one he liked, he gobbled it up. If it wasn't one he liked, he wrapped it up again, put it back and tried another.

Then he saw the little hillocks of tuna fish sandwiches – his favourites. He piled up a plate and began to swallow them.

'Uh, uh, uh!' grunted Grandpa Leicester disapprovingly, swooping out of nowhere. 'Greedy boy! You know the rule. FHB.'

'What's FHB?' asked Sanjay gloomily.

'Family Hold Back, of course. Look after your guests first. Come now, hand round the sandwiches like a good boy.'

'I thought I was a guest,' muttered Sanjay under his breath, as he passed among all the guests, offering them the tuna fish sandwiches, which he loved, and was dying to eat. When no one was looking, he rushed back to the dining room, piled up his plate and dived under the table.

Neetu spotted the Ambala sweets. She loved Indian sweets and was about to select a pistachio-flavoured one, and a carrot burfi, when Grandpa Leicester passed by.

'Uh, uh, uh!' Grandpa Leicester caught her red-handed. 'Have you eaten anything savoury yet?'

'No, Grandpa.' Neetu shook her head guiltily.

'You know the rule,' said Grandpa Leicester sternly, 'savoury first, then sweet.

But first, here, be a good girl and pass round these chicken drumsticks.'

Dutifully, Neetu passed round the chicken drumsticks, but as soon as no one was looking, she rushed back to the dining room, piled up her plate with Indian sweets, and dived under the table.

Grandpa Chatterji wandered into the dining room. 'I wonder where my grandchildren are,' he murmured out loud, and thought he heard a giggle from under the table.

An hour went by, maybe two. Then Mum wondered where the children were, and where was Grandpa Chatterji? 'Have you seen Grandpa Chatterji?' she asked Dad. 'And I can't see Neetu or Sanjay.'

'I'll go and look for them,' said Dad, and disappeared.

A lady bustled through the throng. 'Have you seen my little grandson Raju?'

Mum shook her head. 'I'm looking for my children too.'

Then Mum heard another voice, and another, all asking where their children had got to.

With a shock, Mum realised that she couldn't see a single child – except for one - little Geeta Gupta, who had only just learned to walk, but who was being held in her daddy's arms. Mum asked them, 'Do you know where all the children have gone? Have you seen my father, Grandpa Chatterji, and my children, Neetu and Sanjay? I can't see any of them.'

Mr Gupta put down his little daughter. 'No, I haven't,' he answered. 'But how are you? It's been a long time! You and your husband must come round for supper one evening.' And so they chit-chatted for a while, until he noticed his daughter had gone. He looked around with alarm. 'Geeta! Where's she got to? Geeta!'

Little Geeta stood before the big, long dining table. It was full of wonderful things to eat: mountains of rice, tureens of curry, platters of samosas, bowlfuls of salads and, best of all, chocolate cakes, jellies, biscuits and sweets. But the table was too high.

Geeta stood on tiptoe, stretched all her fingers out as far as they could go. But no matter how high she stretched, and no matter how far she reached, she could not get at the goodies on the table. As she stood there disappointed, a hand appeared from under the table and gave her a piece of chocolate

cake. Geeta bent down with astonishment. Who was under the table? She dropped to her knees and . . .

'Everything all right?' Grandpa Leicester

asked his guests. 'I hope you are looking after yourselves – having plenty to eat and drink, eh?' But something was strange. All the children had vanished. He couldn't see his grandchildren, Neetu and Sanjay, and he couldn't see Grandpa Chatterji.

He had a sudden horrible thought and rushed away to the kitchen. 'Maybe he's cooking. Grandpa Chatterji must have been a cook in his previous life. Can never keep him away from the kitchen!' he growled.

But no – Grandpa Chatterji was not in the kitchen.

'I'll go and search in the garden,' he thought. 'There'll be trouble if they've been running through my flower beds.'

But they weren't in the garden.

Grandpa Leicester frowned. Where was

Grandpa Chatterji? After all, he was supposed to be Chief Guest. 'What an incorrigible man he is,' he snorted. And where were all the children? They were supposed to be offering the guests plates of nibbles.

He decided to do a tour of the house, in case they were all upstairs. But no, they weren't upstairs. When Grandpa Leicester came down again, more of his guests were wandering about looking for their children. He felt extremely annoyed. 'Why can't parents control their children? They are so badly brought up these days!' he muttered. Something was going on, and he didn't know what – even though this was his own party. He felt cross and left out.

He wandered into the dining room. He

would comfort himself with some of his favourite Ambala sweets. But he couldn't see them anywhere. Then he decided he'd make do with a chocolate from the large golden box. He opened the lid. Every single chocolate had a little bite out of it. 'Sanjay!' he bellowed.

Suddenly he heard a soft sneeze and a

stifled giggle. It seemed to come from under the table. He lifted up the edge of the tablecloth and bent down to investigate, and . . . 'What on earth . . .!' Grandpa Leicester looked as

if he would explode.

There, under the table was Grandpa Chatterji beaming up at him, surrounded by Neetu, Sanjay, Geeta and all the other children. It was like a house within a house; a house under the table. Spread before them were plates of sandwiches, samosas, crisps, nuts, chocolate biscuits and his favourite Ambala sweets.

'Come, come, come!' whispered Grandpa Chatterji.

'Don't be ridiculous! I'm not crawling under the table. Come on out immediately,' commanded Grandpa Leicester.

'Come sir, sit, sit!' Grandpa Chatterji patted the floor, and he smiled a beautiful smile. 'I'm telling everyone a churning story.'

'What's a churning story?' asked Neetu.

'They're stories which came out of the churning of the milk, when the universe was formed,' replied Grandpa Leicester, forgetting he was angry.

'This one's about Garuda, the eagle, who saved the world,' explained Grandpa Chatterji.

'Oh!' sighed Grandpa Leicester, 'that's one of my favourites,' and suddenly he remembered how his grandfather had told him churning stories about the creation of the universe. He felt like a child again. Could he . . . would he . . .? He got down on his knees, even though he was wearing his best suit.

'Here, here, sit here, Grandpa,' murmured Neetu, and she beckoned encouragingly. Grandpa Leicester crawled under the table.

'Would you like one of Grandpa Chatterji's pakoras?' asked Neetu politely, holding them out. 'They're very good.'

'Hmm! They were supposed to be for me,' grunted Grandpa Leicester, popping first one, then two into his mouth.

'Would you like a chocolate?' asked Sanjay, holding out a hand with one of the chocolates from the box.

'So that's where my chocolates went,' grunted Grandpa Leicester, and popped two into his mouth. 'Carry on, carry on,' he ordered.

'You see . . .' Grandpa Chatterji

continued, 'Lord Brahma had been asleep, lying on a lotus flower and floating on a sea of milk. He had been sleeping for thousands of years, and when Lord Brahma sleeps, the world doesn't exist. But when he wakes up, then he starts his creation all over again.

'Lord Brahma woke up. He got to his feet and began to stretch. He stretched arms upwards this way . . .' Grandpa Chatterji stretched his arms, 'and he created the sky, he stretched down to his toes, and created the earth, he stretched out, this way, and created the sun, the moon and stars, and he stretched that way and created the winds, the rain and

snow. Soon, with all his stretching, he created mountains and deserts, seas, forests and rivers, and then he created all the animals and birds and fish; all the slithery creatures, those that swung and crawled and sprang and swam, and at last, he created the angels in the heavens and the demons in the bowls of the earth.

'From out of the sea of milk, there rose a great mountain and, coiled around this mountain was a mighty serpent, which had a deadly poison, and could destroy the world,' said Grandpa Chatterji, in a voice full of awe. 'The angels rushed over to the serpent and grabbed its tail to unwind it from the mountain, but the demons flung themselves on to the serpent's head. Soon, there was a deadly tug of war, as the angels and demons pulled the serpent this way and that. The churning began.

'Their pulling made the mountain spin. The spinning became a churning, and the sea of milk was whipped until the milk began to solidify and turn to butter.

'From out of this churning, all sorts of wonderful things rose into being; gods and goddesses, the tree of paradise, and all the sacred animals; a marvellous cow, a white horse for Lord Vishnu, an elephant for Lord Indra and a lion for the goddess Durga.

Most wonderful of all was when the goddess Lakshmi appeared, sitting on a lotus flower, with her four golden arms outstretched.

'"Behold, my queen!" exclaimed Lord Vishnu.

'"Oh no!" shrieked the demons. "She must be ours!"

'Now began a battle for the soul of the earth – a battle between good and evil. As the angels and demons continued to churn the milk, a glistening moisture settled on the butter-like surface of the newly created world – the sort of moisture you see on freshly made butter. They knew that this moisture was holy and precious, and that anyone who drank it would live for ever.

'The angels let go of the serpent's tail and rushed for a cup and filled it with the life-giving moisture called soma. But so did the demons, and in the struggle they got hold of the cup for themselves. Would evil win and take over the earth? No! Suddenly, there was Garuda, the Eagle. He was on the side of the

angels. He knew, that if the demons succeeded in drinking from the cup they would live for ever, and everything would be bad. Like a streak of lightning, he flew over and snatched up the cup with his talons, and flew away.'

'Like my kite,' whispered Sanjay excitedly.

'Don't forget what happened next, after Garuda flew away,' urged Grandpa Leicester.

'Ah yes,' nodded Grandpa Chatterji. 'To take revenge, the demons hissed and cursed, and the throat of the demon serpent swelled with poison. If they couldn't control the world, they would destroy it. The serpent shot out his fiery tongue, and with it came a vast spurt of blue poison. If the poison had fallen on to the earth, Lord Brahma's creation would have been destroyed. Lord Shiva saw the danger. He sprang over with open mouth. The burning, blue venom poured down his throat and he swallowed it.

'That's how the world was saved, and

that's how Shiva got his blue throat. He became known as "Nilkanth", The Blue-Throated One.'

Mum had been hunting everywhere, but there was no sign of Neetu and Sanjay, nor Grandpa Chatterji, and when she looked for Grandpa Leicester, she couldn't see him either. 'What's happened to everyone?' she asked Dad. 'Where have they all gone?'

'Your father's probably taken them off for a ride on a magic carpet,' Dad joked grumpily.

'We'd better start searching,' said Geeta's dad, and everyone agreed.

They too searched all round the house, all round the garden, over the fence into next door's garden, and even outside the front door. But there was no one.

Once again, they went to the dining room. Most of the food had disappeared. All the pakoras had gone, the chocolates had gone, the Bombay Mix had gone, and all the Ambala sweets too. 'Nearly all the food has gone!' cried Mum. 'Who's eaten it all?'

Suddenly, Dad saw a hand coming out from under the table. Its wrist came out of a sparkling white shirt sleeve with a stiff, smart cuff held together with a diamond cuff-link.

The hand flapped about, reaching for something. It found a plate with the remains of some fairy cakes. The hand slid the plate towards the edge, then it disappeared under the table.

'What on earth is going on!' cried Dad, dropping to his knees.

Everyone else got down on their knees too, and looked under the table.

There were the children. They looked up, their eyes wide with excitement, their cheeks

bulging with fairy cakes. And there were the two grandfathers.

'Shush!' whispered Grandpa Chatterji, putting a finger to his lips. 'We're just getting to the end of this story. Come and join us.'

Grandpa Leicester put a finger to his lips and frowned at them to keep quiet, then he stuffed another pakora into his mouth and nudged Grandpa Chatterji to continue.

Then Mum and Dad shrugged, and crept under the table. The other guests looked at each other and shrugged, then they too crept under the table.

'Garuda flew all the way across the world, and sometimes, little drops of soma splashed out of the cup. Everywhere a drop fell became a holy place in India, and when Brahma created people, they built temples and thanked God for creating such a beautiful universe.'

Grandpa looked up beaming. 'Now, have you all tried my pakoras?' he asked, snatching the plate from Grandpa Leicester. 'You'd better have one quick, before Grandpa Leicester eats them all up.'

Everyone took one, and complimented Grandpa Chatterji on being such a magnificent maker of pakoras, and for keeping their children entertained with such a good story.

At last it was time to go home. 'What a fantastic party it was!' they cried. 'The best ever! Never spent a party under the table before.'

As Mum, Dad, Neetu, Sanjay and Grandpa Chatterji all piled into their car,

Grandpa Leicester gave each of them a hug. He even hugged Grandpa Chatterji, and murmured in his ear, 'Well, old chap! You should do this again some day!'

'Tell us a story on the way home, Grandpa!' begged Neetu and Sanjay.

'Yes!' beamed Grandpa Chatterji. 'Now, what about the story of the first man called Manu, who was told by a fish to build an ark and save the world from a terrible flood?'

'Oh! I wish you'd tell it to me too,' sighed Grandpa Leicester. 'I love that story. Oh well, next time,' and he waved and waved as the car pulled away. He was still waving when it turned the corner at the bottom of the road.

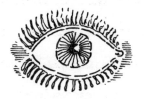

Follow the Brolly

'Bed Tea!' sang Grandpa Chatterji,
balancing a tray in one hand, while opening
the bedroom door with the other.

Mum and Dad were still dozing, but
they had got used to Grandpa Chatterji
waking them up in the morning with a cup
of tea, though Dad always gave a groan,

just to make the point that he'd rather go on snoozing.

This morning Grandpa hopped like an imp as they sipped their tea sleepily. 'I'm making breakfast,' he announced in a chippy voice. 'I haven't had a good old chilli omelette and a nice thick paratha since I left India. Not that I don't love your English breakfasts,' he said reassuringly, as Mum looked at him with a baleful eye. 'I love eating your cornflakes and frosties, or your steaming bowls of porridge. I love eating your fried eggs and bacon, followed by toast and marmalade. But today, I feel like an omelette with fried onions and two hot chopped chillies. I've rolled the dough to make the paratha, and I hope it will make you remember how much you used to love eating parathas and honey. Eh?' He leaned over and patted his daughter on the head. 'Another cup of tea?'

'Uh mmmm,' grunted Dad, rolling over like a sleepy hedgehog. 'No thanks.'

'Yes please,' smiled Mum, and her father poured her a second cup, then marched off downstairs to make his Indian breakfast.

Neetu and Sanjay had got up, and soon Mum and Dad, too, came downstairs. They were hungry. Where was breakfast?

Suddenly, there was a wail of impatience in the kitchen. 'Where the devil is Mrs

Fernandez' Pickles?' bellowed Grandpa Chatterji. 'I've found the HP sauce, the tomato sauce, the mango and lime, the brinjal pickle, the sweet and sour, and the piccalilli – but I'm blowed if I can find Mrs Fernandez' Pickles. Where do you keep it?'

'But, Pa,' cried Mum, hurrying into the kitchen, 'you can't get Mrs Fernandez' Pickles here.'

'Of course you can,' Grandpa insisted. 'Mrs Fernandez' Pickles is found all over the world. Why, I know someone who bought a jar in Dar-Es-Salaam, and Cape Town, you can buy it in Hong Kong and Singapore. I don't believe you can't get it here.'

'Believe me, you can't,' said Mum softly. 'Now, come on, just make the omelette – here are the onions and chillies.'

'I'm not eating any omelette unless it's accompanied by Mrs Fernandez' Pickles,' declared Grandpa Chatterji forcibly.

'Oh well! It's toast and cornflakes – come on everyone!' cried Dad.

'Forget it, Pa,' Mum begged her father. 'Have some breakfast, and we can go shopping later and see what pickle we can find for next time.'

'No, no, no! You eat up. I shall go and look for a jar of Mrs Fernandez' Pickles.'

'I'm going too!' yelled Sanjay, swallowing the last mouthful of cornflakes, and grabbing a piece of toast dripping with honey.

'Me too,' cried Neetu, leaping down from the table.

'Get back to the table,' roared Dad.

'Don't you dare leave till you've finished eating.'

'I'll wait, dearies,' smiled Grandpa, suddenly serene. He had put on his coat and a muffler round his neck, but now, sat down in the middle of the floor, closed his eyes, and balanced his brolly across the palms of his hands.

'Oh, Pa,' sighed Mum, sitting down to her bowl of cornflakes. 'Where do you think you'll go?'

'We'll start at the supermarket.'

'Let them go,' murmured Dad. 'At least we'll get some peace, and I can watch the cricket.'

So Neetu, Sanjay and Grandpa Chatterji set off for the supermarket, in search of Mrs Fernandez' Pickles.

Grandpa Chatterji plunged into the supermarket. He raced up and down the aisles looking for the pickles. He snatched at this jar and that jar, he looked in this section and that section, he even looked in sections where you shouldn't really find pickles like the ice-cream freezer and the cake mixes, just in case someone had put it in the wrong place. But nowhere could he find a jar of Mrs Fernandez' Pickles.

He asked an

PICKLES
CHUTNEYS
SPICES

assistant. 'This is the biggest, greatest supermarket in all the UK, is it not?' demanded Grandpa Chatterji.

'Quite right, sir,' agreed the assistant. 'We pride ourselves on having almost everything our customers require.'

'Then please, I am asking you, where can I find a jar of Mrs Fernandez' Pickles?'

'Whose pickles?' The assistant frowned.

'Mrs Fernandez. She makes the best pickles in the world,' cried Grandpa.

The assistant hurried off to find his supervisor, who hurried off to find his list, and then when they couldn't see Mrs Fernandez' Pickles listed on the sheet, went to the computer to see if it was stocked in any of their warehouses.

At last they returned, looking very

solemn. 'So sorry, sir. We have searched everywhere, but we cannot find any mention of Mrs Fernandez' Pickles.'

'Oh dearie me,' sighed Grandpa Chatterji.

'Are we going to give up, Grandpa?' asked Neetu.

Grandpa had gone silent. He hung his brolly from his wrist, he lifted one leg and tucked it behind the other like a heron, he shut his eyes and put the palms of his hands together, and breathed deeply.

'Is he all right?' asked one

of the assistants.

'He's just thinking with his third eye,' explained Neetu.

'Oh, I see. Then I don't suppose you'll be needing us any more. Sorry we couldn't help,' and they hurried away.

The children waited. What was Grandpa seeing? Suddenly, he stood on two legs, and grasped his brolly with two hands. It swivelled, and seemed to tug Grandpa in the direction of the exit.

'Follow the brolly!' yelled Grandpa Chatterji.

'Follow the brolly!' cried Neetu and Sanjay, and they all rushed out of the supermarket.

'Where are we going?' demanded Neetu, as she grabbed on to Grandpa's waistcoat.

'We're going to find a jar of Mrs Fernandez' Pickles,' chortled Grandpa.

'But where?' shouted Sanjay, grabbing Neetu's hand.

'I told you, follow the brolly!'

They followed the brolly along the High Street. They reached the zebra crossing, the traffic stopped. They swept across. The brolly jerked to the left. 'Where are you going?' yelled Sanjay's friend Ross, who was shopping with his mother. 'Follow the brolly!'

cried Sanjay. Ross grasped Sanjay's hand.

'Where are you going?' cried Ross's mum, trying to pull him back.

'Follow the brolly,' cried Ross.

'We're going to find a jar of Mrs Fernandez' Pickles,' cried Neetu. 'Grandpa says it's the best.'

'I'd better come too, then,' cried Ross's mum.

Grandpa was striding away now, and all the others had to run to keep up with him. They passed the black cat on the wall. He arched his back and waved his tail, to show he wanted a stroke, but they all rushed by.

'Sorry, pussyji, we're on our way to find a jar of Mrs Fernandez' Pickles,' gasped Sanjay, 'and we must follow the brolly!'

The black cat leapt off the wall and

began to follow them.

'Tibby, Tibby, Tibby,' called old Mrs Peabody, who owned the black cat. 'Where are you going?'

'We're off to look for a jar of Mrs Fernandez' Pickles,' cried Ross's mum. 'We have to follow the brolly.'

'Wait for me,' pleaded old Mrs Peabody. 'I love pickle, and I mustn't lose Tibby.'

The brolly whirled in Grandpa's hand and made him turn right, then left, then right again.

Old Mr Desai was sitting on a bench with his wife, enjoying the sunshine, when round the corner charged Grandpa Chatterji, Neetu, Sanjay, Ross, Ross's mum, the black cat and Mrs Peabody.

'Oh!' exclaimed Grandpa at the sight of

a fellow Indian and his wife. 'Good day to
you, sir, madam!' and he bowed very low,
closing the palms of his hands together in a
namaste. 'We are in the process of looking for
a jar of Mrs Fernandez' Pickles. I am hoping
very much that we are on the right track.
Does it ring a bell?'

'Mrs Fernandez' Pickle?' Mr Desai

frowned. 'Goodness me. How you take me back to the good old days. We used to get Mrs Fernandez' Pickles in Pune, but not here. You won't find it here,' said Mr Desai, and his wife nodded in agreement. 'No, no, no! Mrs Fernandez' Pickles comes from Pune. You won't find it here in the UK. Oh, what a favourite it was though. We never had an omelette without Mrs Fernandez' Pickles back in India.'

'Quite right, quite right,' clicked Grandpa Chatterji, 'but I know you can get it here. I know we are very near. My brolly says so.' Then Grandpa Chatterji stood on one leg, slid the brolly on to his wrist, put the palms of his hands together and closed his eyes.

'It's all right,' explained Neetu. 'Grandpa is seeing with his third eye.'

'Ah! Yes, of course,' nodded Mr Desai, understandingly, as Neetu, Sanjay, Ross, his mum and Mrs Peabody all did the same.

The black cat purred, and set off down the road alone.

The brolly flipped on Grandpa's wrist and nearly pulled him over. 'My cat's on to something,' cried Mrs Peabody, opening her eyes. 'Follow the cat!'

'The brolly wants to follow the cat! Come on, we're nearly there!' chortled Grandpa.

'Follow the brolly!' shouted the children.

'Can we follow too?' asked Mr and Mrs Desai.

'Of course! We all love Mrs Fernandez' Pickles!' shouted Grandpa Chatterji.

A run-down little shop shivered on the corner

of Bottley Street and Marsden Grove. It was called Anand's Grocery Store. Its dusty windows were plastered with advertisements for cut-price ketchup, fish fingers and cat food.

The black cat sat outside, and licked its chops.

Up trooped Grandpa Chatterji, Sanjay, Neetu, Ross, Ross's mum, Mrs Peabody and Mr and Mrs Desai.

'This doesn't look very promising,' Mr Desai shook his head. 'Why, he doesn't even sell lime pickle.'

'We've got used to tomato ketchup,' sighed Mrs Desai.

'Well, at least little Tibby knew this shop would sell his favourite cat food,' laughed Mrs Peabody.

'And I like fish fingers!' cried Ross.

'Oh dear,' Neetu said sympathetically. 'Poor Grandpa did so want a jar of Mrs Fernandez' Pickles to eat with his omelette.'

Grandpa stood on the threshold of the shop. His brolly was clasped in his hands, and it pointed up to heaven. 'We've arrived,' he whispered. He pushed open the door, and a bell clanged loudly.

'Yes? Hello? Can I help you?' a voice chimed out of the gloom behind the counter. There stood a very small, very old man

wearing Indian-style pyjamas, with shirt and waistcoat, and a pair of spectacles balanced on his nose. It was Mr Anand.

'Do you happen to have a jar of Mrs Fernandez' Pickles?' asked Grandpa Chatterji.

'Mrs Fernandez' Pickles?' A strange smile hovered over the old shopkeeper's lips. 'That was my favourite pickle when I was a child. I couldn't eat an omelette without a good dollop of it on the plate. When I came to England, many years ago, I tried so hard to stock this pickle, but so few people asked for it and, gradually, I had to stop ordering it all the way from India. I haven't had a jar for ages.'

Grandpa Chatterji stood on one leg and closed his eyes. The brolly swivelled round and round the little shop. It scanned the shelves, which were piled with tins of peas and beans, carrots and new potatoes, it swept over the freezer, with frozen chips and cod steaks and pizzas, it probed along the top where there were strange boxes of biscuits and cream crackers, and down to the stacks of crisps and nuts and bars of chocolates. Then suddenly it tugged Grandpa towards the back of the shop.

'My brolly is telling me that you have a jar of Mrs Fernandez' Pickles at the back of your shop,' explained Grandpa.

'Really!' exclaimed the old shopkeeper, taking off his spectacles and polishing them on his shirt. 'As much as I have the greatest respect for your brolly, I'm afraid it must be mistaken. I most certainly do not have a jar of Mrs Fernandez' Pickles at the back of my shop. It's true that I have just had a delivery of sweet mango chutney, but that's all.'

'May I be so bold as to ask your permission to take a look at your order of sweet mango chutney?' Grandpa requested politely.

'Indeed you may, good sir, though I fear it is all a bit of a jumble at the back. I have to do everything myself these days since my wife died.'

Grandpa Chatterji followed the brolly through a bead curtain and into the back of the shop. Sanjay crept in too.

'Hold my brolly.' Grandpa put the brolly in Sanjay's hands, then got down on his knees to examine the crate of mango chutney.

He took out every single jar, and put them back again. 'Oh dearie me,' he sighed. 'My brolly is not usually wrong about these things.'

'Grandpa!' Sanjay yelled. The brolly was jumping in his hands and pulling him into a corner where there was an old shelf full of boxes.

It was pointing up – too high for Sanjay to reach, too high for Grandpa, and much too high for Mr Anand.

'Have you a ladder?' asked Grandpa excitedly.

Mr Anand brought a ladder.

Grandpa leapt up the ladder, while Mr Anand held it steady. 'Where is it pointing, Sanjay?' cried Grandpa.

'A little to your right, no, too far, back a bit, up a bit, left a bit. STOP!'

Grandpa's hand hovered over an old

wooden box on the top shelf. 'May I?' he asked Mr Anand.

The shopkeeper shrugged. 'There's nothing in it.'

Grandpa handed the box down to him, and descended.

In came Neetu, Ross, Ross's mum, Mrs Peabody, and Mr and Mrs Desai. They didn't say a word. They just looked as Grandpa prised open the wooden box.

'Ahhhh!' He lifted out a very old, darkened, dusty jar. He held it up to the dim light and read out loud the faded oily words 'Mrs Fernandez' Famous Pickles'. He sighed as if he had glimpsed paradise, and held it against his chest. 'Aaaaaah!'

'Extraordinary!' murmured Mr Anand.

'Now we can have breakfast!' cried

Grandpa triumphantly. 'Come, come! Let's all go home for omelette and parathas, and we shall all experience the delights of Mrs Fernandez' Pickles.'

The shopkeeper said, 'Can I come too?'

'Of course! We must all celebrate together!'

So Mr Anand locked up his shop, and followed Grandpa Chatterji, Neetu, Sanjay, Ross, Ross's mum, Mr and Mrs Desai, Mrs Peabody and, not forgetting Tibby, they all trooped home.

'Put the kettle on for some more chai!' cried Grandpa, when Mum opened the door. 'We have visitors!'

'Oh no!' groaned Dad under his breath. 'I wanted to watch the cricket.'

'Oh!' Mum gulped at the sight of all

those people. Then, remembering her manners, she said, 'Come in, come in!'

'You can all watch the cricket while I make omelette and parathas,' declared Grandpa Chatterji.

'Did you????' asked Mum in disbelief.

'We did!' beamed Grandpa Chatterji, holding up the jar of Mrs Fernandez' Pickles.

'We followed the brolly!' cried Neetu and Sanjay.

'And it brought them to my shop,' added Mr Anand.

'Oh come in! Welcome!' beamed Mum with delight, patting Tibby who sidled in after them.

While Ross, his mum, Mrs Peabody and Mr and Mrs Desai and Mr Anand all sat down with Dad to watch the cricket,

Grandpa rushed into the kitchen to make his omelette and parathas.

Mum took the dusty, ancient jar of Mrs Fernandez' Pickles and looked at it with awe. She tried the lid. It was firmly closed. 'Oh well – I suppose pickle lasts for ever. Goodness knows how long that has been sitting on a shelf.' The lid opened with a pop, and a glorious, spicy aroma rose from the jar. She got a bowl and spooned it out.

'Here we go again!' proclaimed a happy Grandpa, marching in about ten minutes later. 'I've made a nice big pot of chai for you to drink while I prepare the omelette and parathas.' He plonked a huge teapot on the table.

Dad smiled. Even though he would rather sleep than be woken each morning with Grandpa's bed tea, which was made with ordinary teabags and milk. Chai was different. Chai was made with tea, cloves, cinnamon, cardamom, sugar and milk, all brewed up together into a hot stewy drink.

'Now come on, children, help me with the parathas,' said Grandpa and he steered Neetu and Sanjay into the kitchen.

It was nearly lunch time when Grandpa Chatterji marched back in, bearing a platter with a huge omelette, followed by Neetu and Sanjay carrying a platter piled high with parathas.

'Breakfast at last!' Grandpa proclaimed.

The cricket was forgotten. Everyone gathered round the table and each took a portion of omelette and a spoonful of pickle – well, Grandpa took several spoonfuls of pickle – and began to eat with a dreamy look on his face.

'Hmmmm,' sighed Dad. 'I have to admit you make a jolly good omelette. Hmmm, the pickle was worth waiting for,' and he stopped being so grumpy.

'To think I had this pickle in my shop all these years.' Mr Anand patted his heart with emotion.

'Ugh,' said Ross, sniffing the pickle.

'Don't think I'll like this very much,' and he pushed it aside.

'Hum.' Ross's mum raised her eyebrows with curiosity, as she put a tiny bit of pickle on her tongue. 'It's very interesting,' and she immediately reached for her chai and gulped it down to take away the taste.

'Errrrr . . .' Mrs Peabody made some funny noises, and her eyes watered, as she swallowed a bit of omelette smeared with pickle. She leaned over and patted her black cat weaving round her ankles, 'No, Tibby, I don't think you'd like this,' she whispered.

'Oh, this is wonderful, wonderful, WONDERFUL,' exclaimed Mr and Mrs Desai ecstatically.

'What shall we do when it's finished?' asked Mum.

'I shall order some more, that's for sure,' Mr Anand reassured her, 'especially because you make a very fine paratha, sir,' he congratulated Grandpa Chatterji.

'You should try his pakoras,' winked Dad.

'They'll taste even better with Mrs Fernandez' Pickle,' laughed Mum.

Sanjay looked at the pickle. He liked the colour; the reddish, greenish, purple-ish look. He spooned a dollop on to his omelette and

thrust it into his mouth.

'AAAAAAAHHHHHHHH!' He gave a terrible, gurgling shriek, and rushed from the room.

Neetu glanced sideways at Grandpa. 'Do you really love it?' she asked ruefully.

'I love it. It sets my mouth on fire! MMMMmmmm,' sighed Grandpa, and he dug deep into the jar with the pickle spoon for some more.

The Third Eye

Grandpa sat cross-legged on his faded rug. His eyes were closed and his arms rested on his knees. His bedroll was all strapped up ready for the journey home.

'Grandpa?' Neetu called softly, peering through the door. 'Do you have to go?'

'Come, come. Sit here on the rug next to

me,' smiled Grandpa, opening one eye.

Neetu crept in and sat down cross-legged next to her grandfather. She closed her eyes and rested her arms over her knees. 'Are we seeing through our third eye?' she whispered.

'Yes,' murmured Grandpa, 'but I am not looking at anything, I am seeing into my soul. I am seeing how sad I will be to leave you, but I am also joyful that you and Sanjay are such wonderful grandchildren. It is only our bodies that will be apart. When I think about you, and you think about me, then we are always together.'

'Grandpa?' Sanjay peeped through the door. 'Can I sit on your rug too?'

'Come, come, sit here,' Grandpa patted the rug on the other side.

'Are you seeing things with your third

eye?' asked Sanjay, sitting down cross-legged and closing his eyes. 'I dreamt about my kite last night. I dreamt I sat on the back of the eagle and flew all the way to India, and landed on the roof of your house. Did I see all that with my third eye?'

'Yes, you did,' smiled Grandpa.

'I wish you weren't going,' Sanjay added wistfully.

'All we have to do to be together, is sit quietly and think,' said Grandpa Chatterji, reassuringly. 'When you think, then your third eye opens – and the whole universe comes into your mind, and distance is nothing. Some people can be together all day and every day, but they never see with their third eye, and they can be as far apart from each other as India is from England. But we know better, don't we? We will think of each other often, and so we'll never really be apart.'

Suddenly, Neetu opened her eyes. She leaned behind Grandpa and nudged Sanjay. 'It's time now . . .' she whispered.

'Oh yes!' exclaimed Sanjay, leaping to his feet.

The children ran from the room, but were back again very quickly.

'We have a present for YOU,' they cried.

Grandpa opened his two eyes and rolled over to stand on his head. 'A present for ME?' he chuckled.

'Sanjay and I made it together,' said Neetu. 'I think you'd better look at it the right way round.' They held out a green box tied up with red ribbon.

'Goodness me,' murmured Grandpa
Chatterji with surprise, and turned the right
way up. 'What is this?'

'It's a memory box!' explained Neetu.
They all sat down together on the rug.

'Open it, open it!' shouted Sanjay.

Grandpa Chatterji took the box
wonderingly. The children watched him
closely as he untied the ribbon.

'Lift the lid, lift the lid!' Sanjay
urged him.

Grandpa lifted the lid. Inside he found photographs of Neetu, Sanjay, Mum and Dad; and he found a poem written by Sanjay.

Grandpa Chatterji
Came from Calcuttaji
We wish he'd stay foreverji
And never, never leave usji.

Neetu had painted a picture of their house and garden, with Sanjay's kite flying over the tree. 'You can show it to Grandma when you go back to Calcutta,' she said.

'What a wonderful box of magic you've given me!' gasped Grandpa.

'There's more, there's more,' Sanjay peered inside the box. 'Look!' He thrust his fingers in.

'Sanjay! Get your hand out. It's

Grandpa's box,' scolded Neetu. But she looked just as excited and keen to see Grandpa find the last object inside the box.

'What is this?'

'We made it,' boasted Sanjay.

'Mum helped a bit,' said Neetu.

Grandpa held up a piece of card cut out in the shape of a dark eye. Stuck in the middle was a small round gold circle for the pupil, on a black  eyeball. Strands of black and red cotton made the eyelashes. It seemed to look right into their souls.

'It's a third eye,' said Neetu proudly. 'Do you like it?'

Grandpa Chatterji held the third eye to his forehead. 'Now, we will never be apart,' he said.

Then he put everything back into the green box, closed the lid and tied up the ribbon.

High above the earth in the aeroplane, Grandpa Chatterji looked out of the window at a vast landscape of clouds. Sometimes they looked like mountains as high as the snowy Himalayas; other times like white fields ploughed into furrows. They looked so firm and solid that any minute, he expected to see a bullock cart pulling a plough, guided by a farmer cracking his whip, move across the landscape. But he knew it was not so. The clouds, which looked so solid, were nothing but air and water. The earth was far, far below, where his grandchildren were – with their feet firmly on the ground.

He took out the green memory box Neetu and Sanjay had given him. He untied the red ribbon and opened it. He smiled at Neetu's painting of their house, and chuckled at Sanjay's poem. The third eye they had made gazed up at him and seemed to enter his soul.

He curled his feet under him and closed
his eyes. His third eye gleamed in his mind.
There was Neetu, growing up to be such a
kind and loving girl, and there was Sanjay
grinning mischievously at him as he chanted:

'Grandpa Chatterji
Please come backerji
Go upside down
Like a sleeping batterji.'

Grandpa Chatterji would love to have
stood on his head right now, but he decided

he'd better not; not in the aeroplane. People might think he was mad.

Somewhere further down the plane, a baby began crying and bawling and fretting and spluttering. 'Bah . . . weh . . . yah . . .!'

'I beg your pardon. Do forgive me. I'm so sorry to bother you.' Grandpa Chatterji wriggled out from his window seat, and eased past his neighbour. He could see a little head bobbing up and down as a baby was passed from Mum to Dad and then back again.

'Bah . . . weh . . . yah . . .!'

'Excuse me,' murmured Grandpa Chatterji, gently looking down at the agitated mum and dad. 'Perhaps I can help. I'm very good at calming down babies.'

Dad looked at Mum. Mum looked at Dad. The baby bawled. The passengers sighed. 'Well . . . if you think you can help . . .'

'I think I can help,' smiled Grandpa.

As he glided down the aisle rocking the baby, he murmured,

'Hush little babyji

Sleep like an angel-ji

Mummy and Daddyji

Love you for everji.'

She gazed into Grandpa Chatterji's face. Her tear-filled eyes glistened like stars, then closed softly. Grandpa Chatterji's third eye saw her floating among the clouds and soon, the whole plane was at peace.

Gently, he returned the sleeping baby to her grateful mother. 'Thank you,' she mouthed silently. Grandpa bowed slightly, with his hands pressed together in a namaste, then he went back to his seat.

'Excuse me, I'm so sorry to disturb you, sorry, sorry, oh dear, did I tread on your foot? So sorry,' and at last, he reached his seat and settled back with a sigh. As he closed his eyes and began to doze off, he could hear Neetu's voice singing in his head.

'Fly away. Fly away,
Dear Grandpa Chatterji,
Over the desert and over the sea.
When you are back
In your home in Calcuttaji,
Remember your grandchildren,
Sanjay and me.'

RECIPE FOR
MRS FERNANDEZ' GREEN
CHILLI PICKLE

Ask a grown-up to help you make this.

Items required:

1 tray lined with paper towel

1 saucepan

1 paring knife

1 500ml glass jar, sterilised

1 saucepan with tightly fitting lid

1 mortar and pestle or blender

1 whisk

Ingredients:

420 mls of green chillis

1 tablespoon black mustard seeds

1 teaspoon cumin seeds

1/2 teaspoon fenugreek seeds

1/3 teaspoon asafoetida powder

1 teaspoon garam masala

1/2 teaspoon turmeric

1 1/2 teaspoons salt

120 ml mustard oil

30 ml lemon juice

Method:

Wash the green chillis and lay out on the paper towel-lined tray to dry in the hot sun or, if you live in rainy England, in a warm oven for 15 minutes.

Remember to get the grown-up to help you with this bit. Put the black mustard, cumin, and fenugreek seeds in a pan and place over a moderate heat. Dry roast them, stirring often until the fenugreek seeds are golden brown. Tip the seeds into the mortar and pound with the pestle until they are powdered. (Or use a blender.) Add the asafoetida, garam masala, turmeric and salt, and continue pounding until well blended.

When the chillis are thoroughly dry, take a sharp paring knife and make a slit in each one lengthways from end to end. Spread some of the spicy mixture over the chillis, and pack them into the glass jar.

In a saucepan, heat the mustard oil until it is smoking, then let it cool for 4 minutes. Add the rest of the spicy mixture and whisk in the lemon juice. When thoroughly blended, pour this over the chillis in the jar and cover tightly with a non-metallic lid. Place in the sun for five days, shaking the jar two or three

times a day. Bring in at night. Now it's
ready to use.

P.S. The pickle gets hotter and hotter over
time.

GRANDPA CHATTERJI

Shortlisted for the Smarties prize

Neetu and Sanjay have never met their Grandpa
Chatterji and now he's coming to stay. What will he be
like? Will he be stern like their other grandpa?

They're in for a shock. Grandpa stands on one leg,
makes delicious pakoras and sleeps in a bed roll.
And he can see poppies when no one else can!

Whatever will Grandpa Chatterji do next?

A funny collection of stories about a very unusual Grandpa.

GRANDPA'S
INDIAN
SUMMER

Neetu and Sanjay are going to India! They're visiting
Grandpa Chatterji and their cousins Rahul and Radha.

India is a colourful, wonderful, noisy place. Neetu and
Sanjay enjoy playing cricket and eating Grandma's
delicious cakes. But it's hide-and-seek with their cousins
they'll remember the most . . .

Whatever will Grandpa Chatterji do next?

A funny collection of stories about a very unusual Grandpa.

More great stories for you to enjoy

Spud Goes Green
by Giles Thaxton

Spud wants to save the planet. It's 1st January and he's decided to go green — and this book is his diary to prove it! The year starts well: he learns to grow food, recycle rubbish and look after wildlife. With the help of Adi and some friends, Spud is determined to give it all he's got, no matter what goes wrong!

Akimbo and the Elephants
by Alexander McCall Smith

When Akimbo sees what poachers do to the elephants on his game reserve, he is determined to stop them. There's only one way to do it, and that's to become an elephant hunter himself! But it's going to take strength and courage, and will involve facing danger

Tilly Beany and the Best Friend Machine
by Annie Dalton

Tilly Beany has never thought about having a best friend. But suddenly everyone has one.
Will Tilly ever find that very special friend who will like her best of all?

Kitty and friends: I don't want to!
by Bel Mooney

NO! It's too early for bed. I WON'T clean my teeth. I SHAN'T tidy my room. I don't want to! Kitty's favourite word seems to be NO!

But soon Kitty realises that saying no gives her more problems than she bargained for!

Captain Fact's Roman Adventure
by Knife and Packer

Whenever disaster strikes, weather-man Cliff Thornhill and his dog Puddles are transformed into Captain Fact and Knowledge. Captain Fact knows pretty much everything about everything and, he has a different gadget for every adventure. You can count on our heroes to save the day, whatever the crisis!

In their latest adventure, Captain Fact and Knowledge grapple with gladiators in Ancient Rome!

Stanley and the Magic Lamp
by Jeff Brown

Stanley Lambchop finds a genie inside Mrs Lambchop's teapot. Now the Lambchops can wish for anything in the world: fame, a magical pet, superpowers…

Being famous is exhausting! Soon everyone longs for life to get back to normal.

But can Stanley reverse the wishes?

See www.egmont.co.uk
for more information on these great books and many others!